# 'Even That Moose Won't Listen to Me

## to Me ❀ by MARTHA ALEXANDER

· Dial Books for Young Readers ·

*New York*

*Summer B. P.*

*Published by Dial Books for Young Readers*
*A Division of NAL Penguin Inc.*
*2 Park Avenue*
*New York, New York 10016*

Published simultaneously in Canada
by Fitzhenry and Whiteside Limited, Toronto
Design by Jane Byers Bierhorst
Printed in Hong Kong
by South China Printing Co.
First edition
1 3 5 7 9 10 8 6 4 2
COBE
Library of Congress Cataloging in Publication Data

Alexander, Martha G.
Even that moose won't listen to me.

Summary: A little girl tries various means to
get rid of a giant moose in the garden after she
repeatedly warns her family and they refuse to believe her.
1. Children's stories, American.
[1. Moose—Fiction.]   I. Title.
PZ7.A3777Ev   1988   [E]   85-4338
ISBN 0-8037-0187-X   ISBN 0-8037-0188-8 (lib. bdg.)

The full-color artwork was prepared using pencil
and watercolor washes. It was then color-separated
and reproduced as red, blue, yellow, and black halftones.

Gregory, come quick! There's a giant moose in the yard!

Who are you kidding, Rebecca? Last week you saw a rocket ship, yesterday it was a two-headed frog. And now it's a moose!

If you don't believe me, smarty, just come outside and see for yourself.

I'm busy, Rebecca. I'm making a scarecrow to keep the crows out of the garden. I don't have time for your silly games.

You better make a scarecrow for the MOOSE or there won't *be* any garden.

Look! Now that moose is trampling the spinach! He might even step on my rocket ship. This is SERIOUS.

Dad, come help. There's a giant moose standing in the spinach! He's going to eat it up!

Sure, Rebecca, when this game is over.

He didn't hear a *word* I said.

I guess we'll just have to chase that moose ourselves.
What will make the most noise?

Look at that moose. He didn't even stop eating.
We better get Mom right away.

Mom, come. Hurry! There's a giant moose eating all the vegetables—and I can't stop him.

What nonsense, Rebecca, you know there are no moose around here.

It is *not* nonsense—it's a MOOSE.
You don't believe your very own child.

If I were big, she would listen to me. When I have a little girl, I'll *always* listen to her.

I have a great idea! I'll put on my hairy monster suit.
That moose will be scared out of his wits!

Hey you, Moose, get out of this garden right
this minute or I'll eat you up!

I give up. He's not even afraid of a monster.
He must know it's me.

Nobody listens to me—not even that moose.

He ate all the vegetables—and
now he's starting on the flowers.
He wouldn't eat a girl and a dog, would he?

Well, *I'm* not going to be a moose's lunch!

Now, listen, Moose, I'm getting really angry!
*Enough* is *enough*. NOW, CLEAR OUT!

Look at that, Homer. He's leaving! He heard me.

GREEEG-O-RIEEEEE! You don't need the scarecrow
anymore. The garden is *all gone*.

Peace at last. Now we can finish our rocket ship.

You just sit on the box so it won't wiggle.

Rebecca, what in the world happened to the garden?

I'm busy now. When I finish building my rocket ship,
I'll tell you all about it.

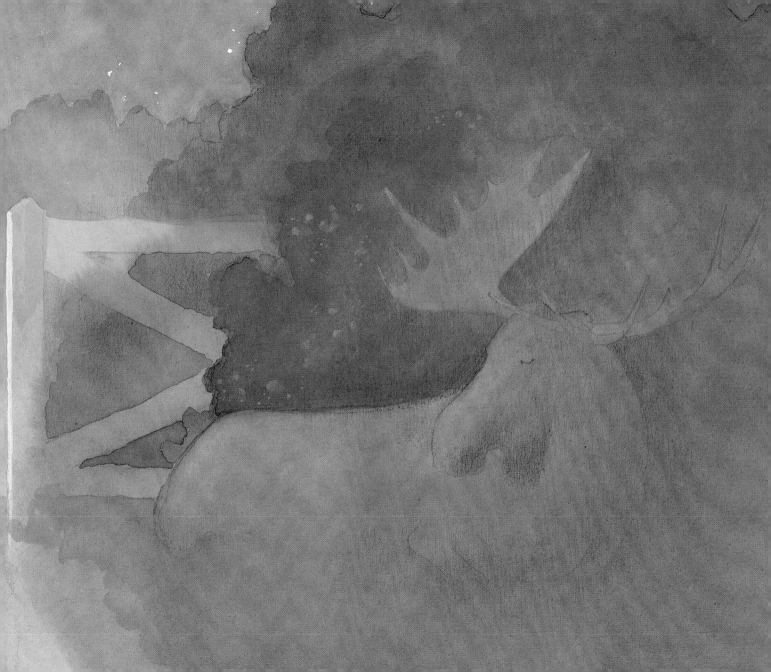